JAMES AND THE WELL

Story by Rob Lee
Illustrations by The County Studio

Fireman Sam was on his way to work one morning when he saw Sarah and James.

"We're going to make a wish in the wishing well at Pandy Farm," said Sarah.

"Why don't you come with us, Uncle Sam?" asked James.

"Why not?" replied Fireman Sam. "I've got some time to spare today."

When they arrived at Pandy Farm, they each made a wish, then tossed their coins into the well. The coins clinked against the rubble at the bottom of the dry well.

"Come on, you two," said Fireman Sam. "If you're quick, I'll treat you to an ice-cream at Bella's café."

"How did you know, Uncle Sam?" Sarah exclaimed. "That's just what I wished for!"

At Bella's, Fireman Sam ordered two large strawberry ice-creams for the twins.

"Thank you, Bella," they said. As Fireman Sam took the money from his pocket to pay, he realised that he hadn't just thrown some coins into the well.

"Daro!" he groaned. "I must have thrown my key into the wishing well!"

"I've got a spare key somewhere," muttered Fireman Sam as he left the café to go to work. "But where?"

"Poor Fireman Sam," said Bella. "It's usually me that loses my door key!"

"Hang on a minute!" said James suddenly. Something in Bella's kitchen had given him an idea. "I know a way we can get Uncle Sam's key back."

James darted out of the door tugging Sarah along behind him.

Firefighter Penny Morris had gone to Pontypandy early that morning. She was showing Station Officer Steele the equipment she carried on Venus, the rescue tender.

"I've got all the latest rescue gear," said Penny. "There are winches, cutters and even an inflatable air bag."

When Fireman Sam arrived, Penny was demonstrating the air bag to Station Officer Steele. Penny pressed a switch on Venus. The bag began to fill with air.

"It's used for rescuing people trapped under a vehicle," said Penny. "As the bag inflates, it lifts the vehicle so we can reach the people underneath."

"Very impressive," said Fireman Sam.

"Humph!" snorted Station Officer Steele. "What's wrong with a bit of old-fashioned elbow grease?"

Back at the wishing well, James was tying a
magnet to his fishing rod. "I got the idea in
Bella's café," he said. "She has magnets on
her fridge to hold important notes."

Sarah could see the key at the bottom of
the well.

"There it is!" she cried.

James played out the fishing line, slowly
lowering the magnet into the well.

"Almost there," he said, stretching over
the well. The line didn't quite reach, so
James leaned over even further. "I've
got —" he started to say, but then lost his
balance and toppled into the well!

15

"James!" Sarah called. "James, are you all right?"

"I th-think so," called back James, his voice echoing around the well.

"I can't reach you," said Sarah. "I'll phone Uncle Sam. He'll know what to do."

"Action stations!" shouted Station Officer
Steele when the message came through at
the Fire Station. "James is trapped in the
well at Pandy Farm! Firefighter Cridlington,
you stay here to mind the phone!"

"I'll follow you!" called Penny Morris as
Fireman Sam and Station Officer Steele
drove off in Jupiter.

17

Fireman Sam drove Jupiter along the winding country lanes. It was raining now, and the roads were wet and slippery. As they came round a bend, Jupiter swerved across the road, skidding on the wet surface, and slid into a ditch.

Penny pulled up alongside as Fireman Sam and Station Officer Steele climbed out of the cab.

"Are you all right, Sam?" asked Penny.

"Er, nothing broken," said Fireman Sam.

"You'll have to give us a lift, Firefighter Morris," said Station Officer Steele as he adjusted his helmet. "We'll sort out Jupiter once we've rescued James."

19

A few minutes later they arrived at the
wishing well in Venus, the rescue tender.

"Don't worry, James," Sam called into the
well. "We'll have you out in no time."

"Fireman Sam and I will lower you into
the well with a rope," Station Officer Steele
told Penny. "Then we'll pull you and James
to safety."

"There's no need, Sir," explained Penny.
We can use the electric winch on Venus."
Penny uncoiled a cable and harness from
he back of the tender and fed it over the
vooden beam of the well. Then she
limbed into the cab and started the engine.
he pressed a button and the cable slowly
owered the harness into the well.

Penny switched off the power and Fireman Sam called to James, "Put on the harness and buckle it tight."

When Sam gave her the signal, Penny switched the generator back on and James was hoisted up the well.

"This is brill!" chuckled James as he slowly rose to the surface.

"Can I have a go, too?" asked Sarah.

"Not likely!" said Fireman Sam as he helped James out of the well. "We'll make sure this well has a grid fitted in future!"

"How did you manage to fall down the well, James?" asked Fireman Sam.

"I was trying to get this back for you, Uncle Sam," replied James, pulling a small metal object from his pocket.

"My door key!" chuckled Sam. "Thank you, James."

24

"That's a very useful piece of equipment, Firefighter Morris," said Station Officer Steele as Penny reloaded the cable and harness onto Venus.

"Thank you, Sir," beamed Penny. "Climb aboard and I'll give you and Fireman Sam a lift back to Jupiter."

As they stopped alongside Jupiter, Station Officer Steele said, "Come on, Fireman Sam, let's get stuck in. We've got to get Jupiter upright somehow. We'll have to go round the other side and push."

"Why don't you try the air bag, Sir?" suggested Penny.

"Nonsense!" scoffed Station Officer Steele "I'm sure we can manage without such contraptions."

Fireman Sam and Station Officer Steele pushed and pulled for all they were worth, but they couldn't budge Jupiter.

"Perhaps we should give the air bag a try," panted Station Officer Steele.

Penny placed the air bag underneath Jupiter and switched on the air hose.

Slowly the bag inflated, pushing Jupiter upright again.

"Bravo!" cried Fireman Sam.

"Hardly a scratch," said Fireman Sam as he examined Jupiter.

Station Officer Steele congratulated Penny as she loaded the air bag onto Venus.

"You're quite right, Firefighter Morris," he said. "There's a lot to be said for modern equipment after all."

"Yes, Sir," said Fireman Sam as he reached into the cab of Jupiter. "But there's one piece of old-fashioned equipment every firefighter should have."

"What's that?" asked Penny.

Sam chuckled as he filled their cups. "A nice, hot flask of tea!"

FIREMAN SAM

STATION OFFICER
STEELE

TREVOR EVANS

ELVIS
CRIDLINGTON

PENNY MORRIS